To Melanie!

To Bangladesh with Love

Andrew Kivistik

Copyright © 2018 Andrew Kivistik.

All rights reserved. No part of this book may be reproduced, stored, or transmitted by any means—whether auditory, graphic, mechanical, or electronic—without written permission of the author, except in the case of brief excerpts used in critical articles and reviews. Unauthorized reproduction of any part of this work is illegal and is punishable by law.

ISBN: 978-1-4834-8592-8 (sc)
ISBN: 978-1-4834-8591-1 (e)

Library of Congress Control Number: 2018906182

Because of the dynamic nature of the Internet, any web addresses or links contained in this book may have changed since publication and may no longer be valid. The views expressed in this work are solely those of the author and do not necessarily reflect the views of the publisher, and the publisher hereby disclaims any responsibility for them.

Any people depicted in stock imagery provided by Getty Images are models, and such images are being used for illustrative purposes only.
Certain stock imagery © Getty Images.

Lulu Publishing Services rev. date: 6/26/2018

Acknowledgements

I would first like to thank my wife Julia for inspiring me to write *To Bangladesh With Love*, and other books. Without her, there would be no light on these pages.

I would also like to thank Bill Halamadaris, my friend and spiritual mentor. Founder of *Heart of America*, he is brilliantly wonderful and author of many insightful books.

Also Shirley Fee Tibbetts, lifetime friend, artist and Creative Director, she has been a compass for me. And Kim Hobbs for the hands-on help and support.

Lastly, friend and photographer Bob McComas for the startlingly magnificent cover photo.

Chapter 1
HER FIRST LETTER.

"If I don't close my eyes I know everything will be alright."
That was the first line of the first letter I received. They are translated but come through with searing vividness.

I thought I understood fear. For me, waking up screaming at 4 a.m. to talk to God with my heart pounding and a day ahead that I am not prepared for. That is fear.

As I slip into this story I realize, I have no idea what fear is.

It was these letters that brought me to humanity. They were the pieces of love I had needed to understand in order to capture the power of hope in a life that seemed doomed. Mine.

Her first letter.

"Dear Julia,

If I don't close my eyes I know everything will be alright. Someone is screaming in the hall and I am so afraid. My pencil is broken and I can barely write. I have a picture of my brother that I keep under my bedroll that I am clutching. It really seems to help me. Right now I am speaking softly to myself just to hear my own voice. That may seem silly but just try it sometime when you are really afraid. I am 7 years old and I am alone and really scared. And…I don't cry.

Bashiri"

Dear God, I think that first letter stopped me in my tracks. Unlike her, I did cry. Yet, I think that first letter just confused me. I thought it would be: "Thank you for your donation, I am happy at school, because of you!"

This is not the case. This girl is real and in trouble.

Well, all is not well in my life either. I was alone too. And I was very afraid of a lot of things — relationships, financial security, family stuff, sometimes even my own sanity.

Mostly I feared a layoff that was rumored to come. It came. Oh, I got some package, but I would be in trouble soon.

Then I got another letter from Bashiri.

Her second letter.

"Dear Julia,

My prayer every night was for joy. This may sound silly, but when joy is missing in your life, it creates a hole in your heart. Although I don't want to, I can feel it. My mom told me.

My mother is out with a man. It is the only way we can survive. When she comes home, she weeps. But she tells me that God will change this for me, that I am an angel.

She also says that when joy is missing from your life, it only means that life is about survival, like the animals. When this happens, you just kind of get numb. Don't let hope crush you. That is why I don't cry. Because I know that if I begin to hope, it will only crush me.

Bashiri"

My dear God, she believes that hope is a dangerous thing. I started thinking about it. It makes sense to her. But what could I do? She is on the other side of the planet and I give $45 a month to make her life easier. I guess it makes me feel good to do it.

Yet I am starting to know this girl. We are both in trouble. And I can see for the first time in my life that her fears are real and mine are just imagined. So I asked her in my next letter to tell me about her life and what a day might be like for her.

Her third letter.

"Dear Julia,

So I begin my day. I walk for 1.5 miles to get water. We have to boil it or we will be sick.

My father disappeared. No one knows what happened. Mom says 'leave it at that.'

So my mom, my brother and I stick together. We pray every night. It is my favorite time. It is the only time we are all together. My brother, Michael is 13 and works at the brick mill. He comes home smelling like a brick, so I tell him so. He just kisses me because we can't bathe here because there is no plumbing. Still, he wipes his face before he kisses me again.

Michael always has spots of blood on his hands. I know that he tries to clean it away, but I see it. We cannot afford the gloves he needs for his job yet. I have promised myself that I will make gloves for him if I can find some material.

We live in an apartment outside Dhaka, the capital city of Bangladesh. The bathroom is outside, but we are used to it. We get clothes from the charity drop-offs in the city square, usually from the United States. I sometimes wonder what it would be like to be there. I hear that they have beds and, …well I should stop. This is what hope is. I can't let myself begin.

We do have a school here. It came with the charity movement and we all can go to age 11.

That is when you go to the brick mill. Michael has friends there. You earn 44 cents an hour. My father worked there before he disappeared. Maybe I will get to work there someday.

Bashiri"

Chapter 2
THIS CHAPTER OF MY LIFE IS EMPTY.

These letters came to me because I am a sponsor. Each word broke my heart in a different place. Sometimes I take the photo off the fridge just to touch it.

I am a divorced woman with no kids so this means a lot to me. What is it about touching things? It just confirms our longing to be together with others.

This chapter of my life is a bit empty right now. Meaning I work very hard at keeping my life together and trying to see the positive side of things. I can see how it would be really easy to fall into darkness. I like helping another girl in a third world country. It centers me in a way that is profound that proves to me in somewhat of a humbling way that I am not really suffering. Yet my heart aches for her, and maybe for me.

I am an advertising account executive. I have a degree in communication arts. I always thought that sounded pretty cool at bars and parties. But the truth is…the real truth is; my life is basically dinner for one every night. And now with the layoff, I am not sure what my next step is going to be.

As I lie in bed, fear covers me like a blanket and I start to cry. Then in an amazing moment in my life …I wonder what it must be like for Bashiri and my tears stop immediately.

I know now what I must do.

Chapter 3
MY BROTHER.

My brother Brian is a dreamer. He has some Internet thing going, but he is basically unemployed. Now that I think about it, he really always has been. But make no mistake he is brilliant. Art, literature, travel, these are the things that help him understand the human condition. He gets it.

So when he said I was crazy to go to Bangladesh. It made me sit back and think it over one more time. Maybe he was right. What am I going to do there anyway? Does it make sense for me to travel half way around the world just so I can hold her hand and give her a kiss? Okay, I am sane again. I will keep supporting her and also begin rebuilding my life. Yes. This is the voice of reason. Then something changed my life forever.

Her fourth letter.

"Dear Julia,

My brother is dead. I can barely write the words. The whole village is crying. I guess Michael went for water. Not the usual way. I don't know, but he stepped on a landmine from a war 50 years ago and he is dead. He was my heart and my spirit. He was my safety when everything seemed wrong. My mother says we are doomed. Lastly, sweet Julia, thank you for helping me. My promise to you is I will never stop trying.

Bashiri"

Chapter 4
IT IS A DARK DECEMBER.

It is a dark December morning in New York. My tiny apartment is a mess. My rent is due.

I have $120,000 I have been saving for fifteen years. My mind is spinning. I look at a stack of laundry and think, "I could just walk out of here." What am I even doing here?

That's when Brian's word came back to me. Yes, he is brilliant. Yes, he understands the human condition. But he is also alive, and Bashiri's brother is dead.

Before I knew it I was on the Internet checking flights. My heart was on fire. I felt alive for the first time since I can remember. My fingers pounded the keyboard like a piano. I was chanting, "I can do this." I found myself smiling with an eager presence of thought. The thought was…I want to give myself to her.

Still, Brian's words lingered. I thought I would sleep on it and make a decision in the morning. So I went to bed and I lay there. As the time clicked by I became more resolute. I thought; "when is a noble decision more relevant in the morning?" I felt my fists clench. As I realized how insane this whole thing was I got up and booked the flight.

The next morning I had the usual sense of slowly coming to consciousness. Then, of course, I startled myself. What the hell have I done? As my heart rate diminished I realized I had a delicious smile on my face. Maybe this was the real me for the first time in my life. I laughed out loud as I shook my head.

Oh, by the way, I did my laundry and I paid my rent but just for that last month. I had a girl to save.

Chapter 5
IT'S 4 A.M.

What do you take to a third world country? I had to get a battery of inoculations, but from what I wondered. There was no way of contacting Bashiri or her family so I decided that from the information in her charity portfolio I would just go and find her. I did not tell a soul.

It is 4 a.m. at JFK. You know that feeling just before a job interview? That is the way I constantly felt. What if she didn't like me or want me? What was I going to do for her anyway? I can't just put her in my carry-on and bring her home with me.

I figured this is how you feel before you get married. It is a kind of excitement mixed with fear. Then I remembered from her letters that I have really never known fear before.

I am on the plane; we are bound for Hamburg. The door is still open. It is amazing to me the things that a person thinks of in the last minute. I could run. My eyes fill with tears as I realize that this has been my M.O. my whole life. "I'm not running," I say out loud as the woman next to me, a bit startled, looks over with an odd expression.

At 29,000 feet, that woman looked at me kindly and said, "what are you running from?" I realized I had turned to stone. I had no idea how to answer her. I smiled in that way when you are mentally absent. She asked again "what are you running from?"

"I guess myself," I said. She nodded as if she understood. Women have a connection like this and it is always a comfort. What it really means is "you don't have to say a thing, I understand your pain, but if you want to say anything, I am here to listen." Men should be so lucky.

I smiled at her and I could feel the force of the tears coming into my eyes. I was paralyzed with emotion. I couldn't speak but I felt the woman's hand come over and touch mine. I am not a weepy person but…and then I suddenly yelled out, "I really love this girl in Bangladesh and come hell or high water I am going there to save her!"

"Oh my God," she said, "tell me all about it."

The flight attendant took our order and soon we were clinking glasses of chardonnay and becoming fast friends. Well, they really didn't clink because they were made of plastic but we didn't care.

Her name was Donna and she lived in Arkansas. I said, "Where is your straw hat and banjo" because she had no accent. She said she had transferred there with her husband to work at the University. She was a Ph.D. and her husband sold motorcycles. "Okay," I said.

Then the smile ran away from her face and she said, "Who is this girl?"

As my mouth slowly began to form the name "Bashiri," my heart stepped in and said it is time to cry now.

Then Donna said, "Some people's destiny just passes by, but I see you are not going to let that happen." She smiled sweetly then looked back to her magazine.

Over the next six hours, we became life-long friends. She gave me the first opportunity to articulate what I was trying to achieve.

Which, at the end of this protracted conversation, gave me a life lesson that came to me later in a dream as we flew across the Atlantic. It was simple… I wanted to exonerate my spirit from a life of meaninglessness.

That is a terrible word: meaninglessness. It just means you get up, go to work, come home, go to bed, and do it all again in the morning. Of course, there are various details in this numbing pattern that give us the illusion of change and maybe we even believe we are making a difference. But when we corner ourselves and say "What difference?" the answer becomes clear and it does not sit well with the hungry spirit that is born in each of us.

Chapter 6
WHERE AM I GOING TO GO NOW?

We had to part in Hamburg, but we vowed to contact each other. She was going to visit her uncle in Estonia and would be back in the states in three weeks. The last few legs of my flight seemed listless and remarkably detached as I missed my friend and anticipated Bashiri.

As we landed in Dhaka, the capital of Bangladesh, I began to realize with hand clenching realism the reality of this third world. I have never seen a major airport like this. It was surprisingly modern, yet planes were swarming everywhere. I was glad to be on the ground.

I guess it was at this moment that I again realized that I had done no real preparation for this visit. Nobody knew I was leaving New York or arriving here, especially Bashiri.

That is where fear sets in. You know that feeling when you start breathing heavily and your heart is racing ….as you sit quietly. The questions start racing in. "Where am I going to go now?" Where is Bashiri's village?" How can I find her and when I do what exactly am I going to do?"

It is easy to get blinded by fear. I stopped myself and prayed. I can't really remember the prayer I said but it was something like this:

"Dear God, I feel foolish and alone. Only with your help can I do this. Please help me find Bashiri."

Then a strange smile came over my face as if it had been answered.

To this day I believe it had.

Chapter 7
I HAD A DREAM I WAS A CHILD.

There is no real "customs" in third world countries. When you give the agent your ticket, it has an American $20 tucked inside. That is just how it is done; do not quote me on this.

As I exited the airport a saddened fear gripped me. "What the hell am I doing here and where the hell am I going to go?"

I remembered Donna saying, "Some people's destiny just passes by, but I see you are not going to let that happen." All right, she's right…I got in a cab.

"I need an inexpensive hotel," I said nervously. The driver, in very good English said, "Madame that can mean many things in Dhaka."

I considered the request again and said, "I need a place I can sleep safely." The cabby laughed and said, "Don't worry, I know just the place."

I arrived at the hotel. I said softly to the cabby, "Will you wait for me so I can see if they have a vacancy?" He smiled widely and said, "They have a vacancy." Then he laughed loudly, yet made an effort to keep it to himself.

I smiled too and thought…this is not Miami Beach. I get it.

They did. I mean have a vacancy. The room was not bad. It was clean and smelled nice. I put my bags down and went to bed. Tomorrow the world would be mine to explore but for now, all I needed was sleep.

That night I dreamed I was a child. The dream was a combination of my childhood with components of my current situation. You know how dreams go, a little bit of fact and a great deal of random neuron firing. This is what I remember. I was in church. My all-American, you know, church. Some lady stood up and said she had brought a friend from another church that had different beliefs. There was grumbling. I guess I was about 6 years old in the dream. I made a grunting sound to participate in the grumbling. But to me, it was just a sound game. Then the lady said she was here with her friend because she had gone with her to her church. More grumbling. I chimed right in. She said, through tender tears that the beautiful thing about faith is that we all get to believe what we need to believe.

I woke up suddenly and with great alarm. It was 4 a.m. local time. I could not sleep. I tried to find some cosmic significance in the dream but I was reduced again to a human being in a giant world. And frankly, I wasn't sure what I believed.

I drew a bath of water to relax. As I gazed in repulsion, I realized the water was brown. A quick call down to the front desk set me straight. "Yes ma'am, the water is brown here." Without thinking my mouth uttered "Okey-dokey." I guess it was right then it hit me, "Dear God, I'm in."

Chapter 8
THERE IS NO WAY TO FIND SOMEONE LIKE THAT.

As I sat in the hotel restaurant that morning, before the food came, it occurred to me this could be any city in the world. Then the food came. Oh, it looked like eggs and toast, but it tasted like something different. As if another culture could examine our food visually, but they would have to figure out what it actually tasted like. It wasn't bad, really. They gladly accepted my MasterCard as if I were in New York. "Maybe things aren't so crazy here." I thought to myself. As I checked with the attendant at the hotel that pleasant point of view began to vanish.

This is roughly how that conversation went. First I must say the woman had excellent English, something I found all over the country. I said, "I am looking for a girl named Bashiri. She is 6 or 7 years old and lives on the outskirts of the Capital city." I smiled back at her as if she could just look into some secret directory of unregistered people and give me her address.

I told her I sent money to a fund sponsored by the U.S. but it just had a code number. She was pleasant to me considering the casual insanity of my request. She calmly said, "There is no way to find people through funds like that." I began to have the sinking feeling that I had done all of this for nothing. She paused for a long time, as if she was deciding if or not she should say what she was about to say. Well, the angels were with me that day, she decided to speak. "I know this man. He can find people. You will have to pay him." I quickly understood that this was a special person and wasn't a regular service of the hotel. "I understand," I said as if I did this sort of thing all the time. "Where can I find him?"

She said in a whisper, "Give me your cell phone number and I will have him call you, it may not be until tomorrow."

Chapter 9
VENKI.

As "tomorrow" rolled around I understood what she meant. I was texted to be at the north corner of what was called Center Square near the Market District. The appointed time of the meeting was to be 10 a.m. — this time had come and gone thirty minutes ago. Then it happened. If it is true that comedy and tragedy live together, this is proof. A school bus pulled up and the door opened… a voice called, "Are you Julia?" There was a long pause as I took in this unlikely spectacle. "Uh, yes." I said and I heard "get in."

This is another of those life moments when your whole body braces and you think it all over quickly.

A great sense of "what really matters" came over me. I got in.

Venki was the bus driver. I mean he was really the school bus driver. He was jovial and round-faced and funny. He had me laughing making fun of Americans and western civilization.

This all took me by surprise with the covert nature of the meeting. I told him my story and he said he did not know Bashiri but he was sure he could find her.

I asked him how much it would cost me. My mind flew through all the extortion movies I had seen. Some time passed. It was a nervous time for me but not for Venki, it was as if he had forgotten the question, he was humming quietly to himself. He finally looked at me and said, "How about twenty dollars?" I felt my shoulders relax; I knew this was a good person. I had a friend and an ally.

He went back to humming before I could make a response. I asked him where he was from, I couldn't place the accent, and he said "the mother country" and went on humming. As I sat back I found myself with a huge grin…"alright" I said, "what mother is that?"

A loud laugh from Venki…then with unexpected gusto… Russia!

Then quickly back to humming. I wondered mindlessly what problem we could have ever had with these people. He was lovely — true and honest and willing to help.

I gave him the money and said there would be more when he found her. It was the first time he looked at me. "Really?" he said. I just smiled and asked him to take me back to the hotel.

Chapter 10
TO FIND THIS GIRL HAD BECOME MY ONLY MISSION.

When I got back to the hotel I decided to stop at the bar for a drink. I certainly deserved it, or so it seemed at the moment. As I lay back I began to realize that this was the biggest thing I had ever done. All the showmanship in my professional life, all the money I had earned, now seemed to be somehow grotesque in the light of the need here. My resoluteness to find this girl had become my only mission. Of course, a small buzz was ok too. I headed towards my room to plan for tomorrow.

As my hand landed on the doorknob, I realized it was ajar. I could feel my heart beating faster. Did I leave it unlocked…no, impossible? I started to turn around when I heard a voice say, "It's okay come on in."

It was Venki. I guess in this country once you become friends anything goes. He was just lying on my bed with a 1990's era laptop. He was wearing a ridiculous outfit featuring a beret and argyle trousers. "I'm getting close," he said with a tone that sent me reeling. "What," I shouted excitedly and louder than I meant to. He looked up a little shocked. "Bashiri attended a school here, at least for a little while." Then he said he could find the records there and packed up his computer and was out the door in what seemed like a second. I think I scared him.

I went to bed with sweet thoughts of Bashiri. The night was loud. I did not sleep well. It seemed that there was unrest out in the street. There was lots of yelling, I could not make it out but I knew something was wrong.

The next morning there was no staff in the restaurant, just the flies from the night before. I waved them away in a wild display of disgust as I sadly realized I would have no meal here. As I looked outside there were no cars.

I went back to my room.

The local TV chatted of the local election, and then suddenly, it happened. It seemed there was civil unrest here for some time. I thought to myself that maybe it would have been wise to do some research.

Then the words came back to me exactly in my father's voice. Just for the record, in my mind's eye, I also saw the furrowed brow I had known since childhood. This gave me strength, my father loved me and he was no stranger to tragedy.

He was a survivor of WWII from Eastern Europe. He did not like to talk about it. But as a child, it fascinated me and as an adult, it gave me a grassroots footing into the human condition. It taught me this: until you have food, the other levels of existence are irrelevant.

The grin reappeared on my face. I had found my anthem.

How dare I worry about myself? My biggest regrets have been things like not being invited to certain advertising parties or regretting not buying the 1000 thread count bed sheets, I settled for the 800.

I actually thought about these things.

I thought about my dad again. I thought about a photo of my dad right after the war. He was really, really thin.

As my head cleared I realized my head was nodding, as if my unconscious mind had already agreed. I called Venki.

As he answered he was involved with a very loud conversation in Russian with another man. Well, you don't have to speak the language to know when people are angry. There was shouting, and I guess the phone was just in Venki's hand. Then I heard a shot. There were more violent screams in Russian and then the phone went dead.

I held on to the phone for what seemed like seconds but were probably minutes.

Chapter 11
SHOULD I COME HOME?

In a fraction of a second, the silence was shattered by my cell phone ringing. I just figured it was Venki. It wasn't. It was Brian. My father had had a stroke. You know that moment when you close your eyes and your whole life seems right there, vivid and real. And at that moment you are asked to bring in an unexpected and dearly unwanted event. As you gasp for breath there is one breath when you just believe it isn't true. But you can only hold that for so long. Then it comes, with the backlash of a lifetime of fear. When it comes to our parents' death, we are all children again and everything in your life stops.

Brian said that dad was ok. It didn't look like there was going to be permanent damage. He could talk regularly and felt good. Brian said he even laughed a little talking about my trip. Normally, I don't know how I would take that, but right now it was a song of joy.

I asked if I should come home. Then Brian said in a 'big brother voice', "What do you think?" I stuttered for a moment.

Then I said with absolute confidence, "my dear sweet bother, you are there to take care of dad, I am here to save a child."

A long silence, then Brian whispered "ok."

Chapter 12
THERE IS NO ROOM FOR FEAR.

I took two long breaths. This was to confirm both that I was not dreaming and that I was really here to rescue a young girl. You know that moment when it feels like a million questions flood your mind, but somehow there is a single resoluteness. By the third breath, I was sure.

I called Venki's number. It rang and rang, and then I got his voice mail. There really is nothing like hearing a man with a thick Russian accent trying to sound like an American. I couldn't help but smile.

Then I remembered the angry voices. I was scared. Then quietly a voice said to me, "There is no room for fear here." To this day I think it was an angel. Anyway, I inhaled another breath and left a message for him to call me anytime, night or day.

Then I said something that even surprised me. I said, "Venki, if you are in trouble, I will help you." Where the hell did that come from, I thought. I'm not here to save everyone in this country.

Then a reality check rolled in …"Like I can save anybody" I said out loud without intending to. All the fears you think you have put away are always waiting to get back in. I shook my head as if I had failed without even trying.

Then, I remembered my angel message from only seconds before and felt a shame the kind I have never known. Not the kind of shame for a mistake, it was different.

It was a feeling that strengthened me and seemed to permanently put away my trivial fears. I was changing. It seemed clear to me at that moment.

The woman I was in New York was not capable of this. I was someone else, and I loved it.

I went back to my room; it was about 5 p.m. local time. Cars were returning to the streets and there were people in the hotel. "Maybe it was Venki who saved the day," I said smiling to myself.

I had started a journal when I left the states but I had only chronicled events, as a third person would witness them. This time I began to write from the heart.

I began to write like the person I was becoming.

The words flooded out of me in a torrent of tears and ink. Maybe in everyone's life there is one thing that they need to do. If that is true I hope everyone gets a fighting chance, because going back to the old you is just giving in to the hopelessness of a dying heart.

I wrote until I fell asleep with my pen in my hand.

Chapter 13
THE CAVE.

I could hear water as I opened my eyes. I was deep in a cave with shallow water. It was very dark but entirely lined with jewels that seemed to glow from an external source.

I could hear a distant voice, a young sweet voice calling to me. As I tried to move toward her I could see the water rising. I could not move my feet.

As I struggled to move, something startled me, I stopped struggling, I was being ripped from the sweet voice, I could feel it, and I could…

It was my phone. I was in my room and it was a dream, a dream more real than I have ever had before.

I grasped for the phone panting as if I had really been struggling. Dear God, it was Venki. He was in jail. He had been participating in a local demonstration and was arrested.

This was the "fighting conversation" I had heard. He said if I came to get him out he would somehow pay me back. "How much will this cost?" I whispered. He said "twenty dollars."

"What is it with this country and twenty dollars!" I laughed out loud and said I would be there to get him. He laughed too but I could tell that his laugh was not real. I better hurry.

Chapter 14
I REMEMBERED THE ANGEL'S VOICE.

I got in a cab and said, "Take me to the police station." The cabby looked at me with a surprised expression and said "Really?" Then he said, "It is called police barracks, you do not want to go there." I rubbed my thumb and forefinger for a moment… "Maybe he's right," insisted my internal monologue. I simply said, "Thank you for the correction, take me to the police barracks and wait for me. I will pay in American currency." A moment passed, he said, "It will be twenty dollars." In that moment, one of those enormous smiles that you cannot control came across my face as I responded, "Of course it will be."

As we pulled up it was not like a police station in the United States. There was barbed wire and guards. It was more like a prison camp. We pulled up to a gateman. The cabby said something I couldn't understand, the guard looked into the back seat at me and smiled with concern marks on his forehead.

We were admitted to drive to the command compound. I was rubbing my hands on my legs nervously as the car stopped. I could see the cabby's eyes in the rearview mirror. He said, "I will wait twenty minutes."

As I got out of the cab I realized I was a bit shaky, and I remembered the angel's voice, "there is no room for fear here." As I inhaled, a shot rang out distantly as if my nerves needed some reassurance that they were really on edge. It made me laugh nervously.

I walked to the poorly lit office noticing there was just one uniformed man within. I knocked on the door and smiled at the officer. To my surprise, he smiled back and greeted me in his native tongue. I spoke in a short English phrase and he answered quickly in kind. I told him my story and who I'd come for.

He told me there was no way he could release a man from this arrest. I told him I had twenty dollars. He said, "Come this way."

In what seemed like three minutes I was in the cab with Venki and we were outside the compound. He was noticeably glad to see me. I guess this type of thing does not happen all the time in third world countries.

The cab dropped Venki and me at my hotel and I agreed to meet him in the morning in the hotel cafe' to make a plan.

Chapter 15
A PRECIOUS BREATH UNTAKEN.

When I got back to the room, there was a fax on my bed with a request to call home. It was from Brian. I could only think it was bad news. I ran for my cell phone, which told me in an unsatisfied tone that it was dead. My hands were shaking as I went through the menagerie of cords on the floor for various devices. I connected the phone at the precise time that it rang. It scared the hell out of me.

With a precious untaken breath, I said hello. It was Brian. Just his voice filled me with so much joy I nearly cried. "Hi," I said so loud it scared me. I only heard "Is that you Julia, I can't hear you…." With all my presence I responded with "Yes it is me and thank God it is you." A moment passed. Then "I can hear you now." I could feel teardrops streaming down my face; there was something about my connection with Brian that fueled my love for life. He was 10 years younger than me. My parents always said he was a "mistake" but to the world that knew him, he was a friend, guide, teacher, and to me a shining star.

His words were shaking. It was not like him. I didn't want any small talk right now. "What's wrong," I whispered. Again there was a long pause. Brian also whispered as he responded. "Dad's gone into a coma."

I could hear him silently crying. I never thought that he and dad were so close. Now I knew.

"Should I come home?" I said with everything I could summon as a stalwart heart. Because really in that moment I knew my family was more important than anything I thought I might be doing here.

Surprisingly, Brian said, "No, you are where you need to be right now, and I have never sensed you so alive." He told me he would give me updates on our father's condition.

As I turned off my phone I exploded into tears remembering all the childhood joys with my father. With three brothers, I was the only girl in the family and I was his princess.

Chapter 16
ARE YOU STAYING OR AM I GOING?

I was flying a plane. It was a single-engine plane and I was trying to gain altitude. But somehow I just couldn't get up to speed. All around me all I could see was water. I tried and tried and then when I saw a cliff ahead, I just landed. I awoke covered in sweat and crying.

I had made up my mind. I was going back home. What was the dream saying to me? I got up and took a shower. By the time I reached the mirror, someone else was looking at me. It was that scared girl from New York. We stood and stared at each other for what seemed like a long time.

Then, I said the most memorable words aloud in my life. "Are you staying or am I going." There was about a second, but within that second I saw my father and my mother as young people, my childhood, memories of grade school, early vacations captured in primitive color photography, vivid images of being at the beach and backyard cookouts, spitting watermelon seeds at my brothers, then it all went black.

I met my eyes in the mirror and said loudly, "I'm staying."

Chapter 17
THE PRIME MINISTER.

I awoke to the sound of my cell phone informing me that it would like breakfast, at least an electric one. It was almost dead, and somehow I felt that too. It was 5:45 a.m. As I came to complete consciousness, I remembered my meeting with Venki.

I have to say something right now. I really like Venki. He is not good looking. But he is not bad looking either. But he is courageous. That is what is missing in the world. Courage. As I write this in my journal, I realize something even more important. It is the cement that has made my life solid for 34 years. The simple truth is: everything is connected and happens for a reason. It occurred to me in an insane moment that maybe I would marry Venki. I laughed out loud and headed for the shower.

We had agreed that Venki would call at 9:00 a.m. Well, nine came …and ten. I started thinking maybe I wouldn't marry him if he were always this inconsistent. Suddenly my cell phone rang. To my surprise, an enormous grin flashed upon my face. "Hello," I said eagerly. It wasn't Venki, it was the maid service, and they would be there in 15 minutes. Thank you, I said in a secretary-of-state voice. I called Venki, but got his voice mail. I was getting hungry and went down to the restaurant.

As I walked in, I was stunned, there was Venki talking to the Prime Minister. I withdrew to the corridor. What do I do? I found myself walking away like a coward. I stopped. I thought, "I am in this thing, I am in it all the way, so I have to be brave."

As I walked up to the table, Venki stood and embraced me. Speaking the native tongue of Bangladesh, he told my story. Now in retrospect, I did not understand a word, but you can tell a lot from a look in a man's eye and the tone of his voice. As the story rolled along I started thinking again that maybe I would marry Venki. The enormous grin returned to my face.

Venki looked kindly at me and asked if I would wait with the hostess for a moment. I smiled and complied. I knew that women in this country must know their place.

As the conversation went on they ordered shots of vodka. This at 9:30 a.m. is not unusual in this land seen through the looking glass of desperation and poverty. After some time, they got up, shook hands and parted.

Chapter 18
TWENTY DOLLARS.

Venki motioned me over. He looked up with a sober expression. In his softest Russian accent he said, "I've got some bad news."

My shoulders dropped. What was all the laughing and merrymaking about I wondered.

Then it hit me. You know that moment of "Oh dear God," when you know bad news is arriving and you haven't heard it yet? That's where I hovered for what seemed like a minute. "What?" I said too loud startling Venki. His eyes flew open wide and said, "It may be nothing." He explained that he had contacted his Uncle … the Prime Minister, to help me find Bashiri. He informed me that according to school record Bashiri had not been attending for at least 45 days.

I sat back and sighed, "Of course not, her brother is dead, now she is taking care of the family." Venki nodded in saddened agreement. "How do we find her?" I said.

Venki looked at me and said, "We must go to the south village, it is where most of the service people live. We can ask around." Then he looked at me with a funny expression. "What," I said softly.

Venki said, "If you have money it will make it easier." "Let me guess," I said "twenty dollars." We both laughed.

By now it was nearly noon and we headed for the south village. Luckily Venki had a cab. There was no charge for this trip.

That's when my phone rang. I could see it was Brian. I began trembling. As I hit the answer button, I just wanted to believe everything was ok.

It was. Dad was awake and a little shaken but was going to be all right. "Thank you," I said through tears as if Brian had saved him. He simply said, "Dad is proud of you for going after this girl." I think that moment stands alone in my portfolio of life. I have a mental snapshot of it that I replay often.

It is the validation from my father that I always longed for. I guess it required me doing something that I was totally afraid of and blindly crashing into regardless of the consequences to get his attention. I smiled a wry smile of satisfaction.

"We're here," from Venki brought me back to the here and now. As we cruised by I could see the shacks made from scraps from the city. Some had windows from automobiles. Almost all had a barrel for cooking, and I guess for staying warm.

We stopped and Venki went up to a woman washing clothes. I heard him say Bashiri's name. The woman looked up quickly then shook her head. We tried several other houses and got the same response. It was easy to tell they were protecting her and her family. After all, they did not know who we were or what we wanted.

I opened my purse and pulled out my magic wand — a crisp American twenty-dollar bill.

This time it was different. We went back to the first woman we talked to. Though I could not speak the language yet, I could see her asking questions before she accepted the money. She looked over at me in the car, I smiled, and she did not. Yet the money changed hands and we had a destination.

You know that feeling when you are trying to get something and you are really focused and driven, and when you finally get it there is a moment of weightlessness when you wonder if you are doing the right thing. After all, it is about to happen.

"Are you ready?" I heard in a Russian accent. I was rubbing my knees nervously yet still delivered with clear comedy, "No, take me back to the airport, I'm flying back to the U.S." Venki looked over to me with the most horrified and beautiful expression I can ever imagine. "Yes," I said, "Of course I'm ready." I saw his enormous eyebrows lower and relax.

Chapter 19
RAPTURE.

As we pulled up the comedy ran away from my mind. This was a shanty. A sort of lean-to, made with cinderblocks and large pieces of industrial roofing. Smoke was coming from within.

Venki said he would take care of it and in a sudden unrehearsed moment I said, "No, I will do it." As I got out of the cab I didn't know what to do or say. I knew I could not understand them and they could not understand me. Yet I knocked on the door.

A handsome woman came to the door and smiled. I smiled back. I noticed she had lesions on her face and arms. We stood there for about ten seconds. Then without control, my eyes exploded into tears and I cried out "Bashiri."

The woman looked at Venki in the cab, who was reading the paper and then back to me. She breathed deeply and invited me in. It is amazing to me that people who cannot speak the same language really can communicate. Especially women. She motioned for me to sit down and brought me some hot tea that was amazingly delicious.

She was gone for quite a long time, maybe twenty minutes and then it happened. I could hear rustling from behind the shack. Then I heard the exchange of words from the woman and a young voice. To this day it is the sweetest voice I have ever heard. It didn't matter that I could not understand the words; I sat in rapture of every sound.

As the rapture passed so did time. Finally, the woman came back in and spoke to me, smiling. I could not understand her but still sensed that she was telling me that Bashiri was getting ready to meet a guest…me.

We smiled at each other for a long time. Surprisingly it was not uncomfortable at all. It was as if she knew me and seemed to understood what I had come for. Then the back door swung open and I saw her. I did not hear the angels sing. I just sat there quietly as she walked toward me. "Bashiri," I said. And her face came into the light and she was smiling. She was beautiful. She was also quite blind.

Chapter 20
AN EMBRACE OF LOVE AND SORROW.

Dear God, I thought. What do I do now? As I began to say my name, I did not know I was crying…she heard "Julia." Her face lit up like a candle and she ran to me. I threw my arms around her and wept wildly. She cried too in a waterfall of mutual exoneration.

I took her by the arms and said, "I'm going to get you out of here." She just smiled at me.

I stood up and motioned for the woman, who I was now sure was her mother, to wait.

I ran to the cab and motioned for Venki to come in. As we sat and talked, we learned about each other. Especially considering what life had been like for the family after Bashiri's brother had been killed. As Venki translated I could tell that Bashiri was quite intelligent and very aware of what was going on. As a woman, I could tell the precise moment Venki told Bashiri's mother that I wanted to save her and take her to the United States. The woman looked at me and slowly smiled through tears and came to me and held me in a way I have never been held since. It was an embrace of love and sorrow.

I vowed to the woman I would educate and raise Bashiri in America and they would be able to be together again, though I knew she could not understand me. With tears that Bashiri could never see, her mother nodded to me and kissed my hand.

I went to Bashiri and ran my fingers through her hair as she repeated, "Julia, Julia" until I could bear it no longer. I grabbed Venki and we left.

As we drove back to the hotel I asked Venki what the lesions were on the woman's arms and face. He said it was a venereal disease, quite common here. "Well, what are we going to do about it?" I yelled. He looked over at me so slowly; it seemed like slow motion and said, "What are we going to do about it? You are saving the world here, I am driving a cab." He took a long breath and said with a deep pain in his voice, "She will be dead soon."

He was sipping casually from a pint of vodka. I looked over and said with my typical American disgust, "Isn't it illegal to drink and drive?" Venki, still in a sad voice said, "Not in Bangladesh." I said, "Hand me the bottle."

I'll tell you what — most Americans, at least like me, don't know what a belt of authentic Russian vodka is really like. Anyway, I spit it out all over Venki's dashboard. He quickly pulled over. I thought he was going to be furious, but he went into a laughing fit that went on for what seemed to be minutes. I guess I even laughed a bit too. I had something to be happy about now. I had a little blind girl from Bangladesh that I was going to love. He dropped me off and we agreed that I would call with next steps. He smiled and pulled away.

Chapter 21
TAKE ME WITH YOU.

The next day I awoke with a fresh opinion and a bright perspective. I went down to the restaurant and had my regular odd-tasting breakfast and saved most of it for Bashiri. I went back to my room and started making calls. First, I called the agency that sponsored me with Bashiri. This was a dead end. It was clear policy that they could not interfere with something like this. I understood. Then I called the U.S. embassy and told them what I wanted to do. I got the usual rhetoric. Basically, they said I had to go through the U.S. based adoption process that usually takes 2-3 years.

I called Venki. This was a man I believed I could trust. So I let my guard down. I asked Venki if he could use his relationship with the Prime Minister to "sneak" Bashiri out of the country with me.

There was a long silence. Venki asked to meet in the Ramna Paric, which is Dhaka's town square at noon. I agreed.

As usual, he showed up at 1:15 p.m. As he sat down I said, "Being this late you would never make it in America." He looked at me with his furrowed brow and said, "funny you should say that."

Again a long silence, then…"I want to go to America, I will help you escape if you take me with you." I started to get a little shaky, but I held on to what I could of the sanity of the moment. "Oh," I said, which sounded a little like

I had not completely thought this thing through. After a moment I said, "Okay, but how?"

Venki smiled as if he had been thinking about this for a long time. "It is going to be tricky, but I think I can arrange some passports, if you can pay." He looked at me and said, "No, it will not be twenty dollars."

This time we did not smile. As we discussed the finances of the affair, I knew I had to wire some money in.

As Venki was driving back to the hotel I said, "What can we do about the disease of her mom?" I saw him shaking his head. "If we make a big deal about her social disease it will expose us."

As he looked at me I was shaking my head, "That's not good enough, surely we could do something anonymously." "Yes," Venki said without any emotion, "but it will take money." I was mad at him for being so cold, but I stayed quiet and just said, "Okay."

By the time he dropped me off, it was evening and we agreed to meet for breakfast and start making our plan.

Chapter 22
MY DREAM WAS IN 8MM FILM.

This time I bypassed the bar and went to my room. I have to get it together I thought. I made a few calls to my Fidelity account; there was another $180K at the ready that could be wired to an account here, should I set one up. I went to bed early and dreamt of the beach. I could see the beautiful waves crashing on the shore. Oddly my dream was in 8mm film and I could see the imperfections in the frames and the lousy color. Still, I loved it. As I moved toward the water something scared me. I did not know what it was. It was like a shadow in the water, huge and moving. Although I was paralyzed with fear, my body kept moving toward the water, soon I was waist deep. I could begin to feel tentacles around my ankles as I walked deeper. Something was coming to the surface, I could see the enormous shadow rising. As it broke the water's surface, I awakened to a soaking sweat and a racing heart.

It was only 10:30 p.m. I decided to go to the bar after all. After a wonderful splash of Pinot Noir, I was headed back to my room when I heard a friendly voice say, "It is early, why not stay and chat?" It was a local man with very good English, and also very good looking. Before I really thought about it, I was back at the bar having a wonderful conversation with this man. He told me he was the Provincial Constable. Which was the highest-ranking police official below the government guys. "Cool," I thought to myself, I am just about to break every law this country has and I am flirting with the chief of police. I started asking basic questions about his job as I batted my eyes just a bit. Then I added a hint of, "How do people get out of Bangladesh?" It was at that point that he looked at me slightly differently. "What do you mean," he said in not a mean way but not friendly either. I took out my passport and said, "I'm just curious." He examined the document and smiled. I could tell he had a lot of stories. Maybe some of them could be helpful.

As we talked into the night he told me of government conspiracies and cover-ups. He told stories of disappearing people and all in the name of the government. "Wow," I said a little diminutively and followed with "What about health care for the underprivileged?" He laughed out loud and said, "Everyone is underprivileged here, and who do you have in mind?"

"Well," I said, "I have seen women with lesions." He looked at me with disgust. "You don't want to know how they got them." I was beginning to see the point of view here. With very limited recourses for medical care, I guess they didn't think it prudent to give first care to prostitutes. It did not matter that it was Bashiri's mother. It did not matter that she did it only for the love of her daughter. These things do not matter in a third world country. Venki's words echoed back to me that I could not save everyone. The night seemed to be getting old so I bid my policeman goodnight. He offered his services, but I declined with a smile.

I had a crazy dream that night. It started out that I was swimming with some dolphins. But then I was a dolphin; I could feel the strength in my body as I glided almost effortlessly through the water. Oddly at the end of the dream, I was ashore with no way to get back to the water. That's when I woke up.

Chapter 23

FISH HERE.

The next morning, I awakened with a new heart. When Venki arrived I greeted him with a hug and kiss. His Russian was undecipherable yet unmistakable. Women know when they momentarily please a man. He ran his fingers through his hair as if he were a teenager. And said, "good morning," with that silly grin men seem to always have after being flattered by a woman. I just shook my head and looked at him, "What am I going to do with you?" His smile vanished; this was not an expression he knew. I raised my hand and smiled, the universal sign of "Don't worry."

I asked him about the passports and how much it would cost. He looked down into his lap and said, "Ten thousand dollars for Bashiri, and two thousand dollars for me." Venki already had a passport, a visa really, but it was expired. "Done." I said in a voice that inspired us both. Grinning we headed off to celebrate. "First, I have to open a bank account here," I said. We stopped at a bank whose name loosely translated into English is, "Fish here." Anyhow, I gave them my account info and in seconds I had thousands of dollars. It was thrilling at the moment, but as I remembered later it was my own money not some windfall. I withdrew fifteen thousand dollars. I gave it all to Venki, we went and had a drink and said goodnight. He vanished into the streets.

I thought with a rush of fear, good God, I just gave fifteen thousand dollars in cash to a man who I don't even know his last name.

The next morning came and no call. I called Venki's cell phone and it had been disconnected. "Oh no," I thought. "Have I just been ripped off?" The next morning came, no call. Then about noon my cell phone rang, it was Venki. He had used 100 dollars to buy a new cell phone and he was happy as a clam. I told him how mad and scared I was and he shut up for a moment and said, "We are in this together, you are an angel and I believe you are doing the right thing. I'm just lucky to come along for the ride." "Alright," I said, "Get your ass over here." I could feel my face getting red. This is not the usual way I speak to anyone. He said, "I'm on my way." My internal monologue said, "Alrighty then maybe I am a bad ass."

As I turned and walked away, I tripped over my feet and decided maybe I'm not a bad ass after all.

Chapter 24
I DON'T WANT TO GO TO RUSSIA.

When Venki arrived I had hot tea ready with some pastry. It is amazing to see the people around here with the simplest things explode into rapture. A look of astonishment was on his face as he inspected the quite modest plate of dessert dishes. "Why didn't you call earlier," he said without really meaning too. "I did." You disconnected your phone. "Oh," he said with a smile as he reached for the pastry. I just sat back and watched. There really is great pleasure in watching another human being have a treat. As he licked his fingers I giggled to myself, which made him laugh to.

After this brief laugh, he looked up with the soberest of eyes and said, "I have ordered the documents for me. I made a mistake about the papers for Bashiri" "What, I said?" He said, "You can buy her passport too, but it will be one hundred thousand dollars." "Dear God," I said. Can I adopt her here? How can we make this easy? Venki looked up with eyes of wisdom, then his eyes turned sad and he said, "You can adopt her here but it will not be recognized in any other country. It would be easier to go to Russia and regroup before going to United States. There it is easy to get papers."

This sent me into a tizzy. I don't want to go to Russia. That sounds like it's own can of worms. "What's another way?"

I looked over with a half smile. "When's the next plane to Russia?" He also looked back with a half smile.

I looked Venki in the eye and said, "I have to discover what is really right for this little girl." Venki said kindly, "I'm not going anywhere." That's when the full smile came to both of us.

I asked him to keep thinking about this and I would contact him in a couple of days.

Chapter 25
I LIVE IN BANGLADESH.

I had to get out of the hotel; it was too expensive for a long stay here. Venki had recommended an apartment near the University of Dhaka. It wasn't much, just one room with a decent bed and a small kitchen. I took it. In an eye-rolling irony moment, I learned it was owned by his cousin, named Vanki. Whaddaya know, Venki and Vanki. Are they a comedy team? Are they short of vowels in the Soviet Union? I guess it is not even the Soviet Union anymore, I just don't know what to call it. "Mother Russia" is not on my list.

Anyhow, I kind of liked the apartment. In an odd moment I realized I had my own place. "Wow, I live in Bangladesh." I went out to get some food. There was a remarkable market on the street just below. Fresh fish, bread, great looking vegetables; we should have it so lucky in America. Then I looked around and realized it was people just like me buying the beautiful produce. This wasn't for the people of this country; it was for the privileged few.

I guess I will hold off on buying a timeshare here. Again I allow myself another half smile. There really is very little room for comedy here. This is the authentic human condition, playing out before my eyes. "You can't save everybody," from Venki has become my mantra.

It is about noon and I realize I need a way to get around without calling Venki for everything. In one of only a few joyous moments, I found myself downtown and I buy myself a motor scooter. The smile on my face matched the enormity of my chinstrap.

I ride immediately to Bashiri's house. Again there is smoke coming from within. I pray all is well. I knock on the door and to my surprise Bashiri answers.

"It is me," is all I have to say before she throws her arms around me.

I know she does not understand English, but she knows my voice. She motions me inside. Her eyes are completely white. Almost no indication of iris or pupil, but they are bright and wide open.

She says something I can't understand. I just take her hands and start humming in a peaceful way. I am crying too but she cannot see that.

I realize right then and there. I will have to learn some of their language called Bangla if I am going to save her and teach her English. I had brought her some candy bars that I put in her hands and told her I would be back.

I think she knew I would.

Chapter 26
THE PRIME MINISTER'S DAUGHTER.

My morning call went out to Venki. "I need to learn Bangla, who can teach me?' He said in a soft voice, "I can." "You're Russian," I screamed laughing. "Yes," he said, "but I'm cheap."

"Really," I said. "I know you know a little, but I need a teacher." I could hear a long exhale on the other end. "I know someone," came a saddened voice. "Venki," I said with joy, "You are the vortex of this whole operation." Venki paused and then said with a beautiful Russian accent, "What is vortex?" I said, "My dear friend you don't even know English, how do you teach Bangla?" "You're right," he said. "I know this woman, she is bartender, but she is also teacher. I will get you number."

Later that afternoon I got a call from this woman. She said her name was Eanna. She did not speak like the locals but said she could teach me the basics of the language in three weeks. I thought she sounded British.

"How much, I said?" There was a long pause, she said, "I am in trouble and I need a place to stay. If I can stay with you and get food, I will do it for free."

This was beginning to sound rotten. I said, "Let's meet in the city square and talk." We agreed upon a time the next morning and where we would meet. As I awoke the next day I was excited. I thought it might be fun to have a roommate. Just like college days.

Well, we were to meet at the fountain at 11:00 a.m. I told her I would have a yellow scarf. Well 11:30 came and went and I thought that Eanna must be a relative of Venki with these habits. As I stood to leave I felt a soft touch on my shoulder. It was not what I expected. She said quietly, "I am Eanna."

She was a beautiful African lady with, I guess, a South African accent. She was looking around nervously. She said, "Let's talk at the café," as she motioned to a spot across the street. As we walked, we did not speak.

We got a table in the sun away from most of the people. As we sat down we both smiled. I piped up, "So you want to be roommates?" She said, "Be quiet. I know who you are and I know what you are doing here." I looked at her and said with that 'I thought I liked you' stare, "Okay, what am I doing here?" She leaned in and said, "You are trying to steal the Prime Minister's daughter." There were weird gears spinning in my brain. I know Venki, he knows the Prime Minister, and we both know Bashiri. What is the connection?"

I looked at her with a mother's eyes and said, "What do you know and why do you know?"

She paused for a long moment. She sat back in her chair. She said, "I know how this must sound strange to you. A lot has happened around here in the last few years. I am here to see that it doesn't get worse."

"Am I doing something wrong?" I said with sure knowledge I was. She said, "You are just a tourist until you touch Bashiri. "How can you even know Bashiri?" I said. Again a long sit back in her chair. "Let me start at the beginning." I interrupted and said, "Can we please get a drink?" Her expression was all I needed as the answer. I could see this was a person of honor and character, what I wondered was how did she find me and know what was planned?

We ordered a bottle of French Merlot. And sat back to watch the sunset and passively turn a page. She explained that she was not an agent; she was a palace protector before the government change. She knew Bashiri from birth and knew she was blind. This birth was to remain private and Bashiri was moved from the palace until she arrived in the arms of her current caretaker. "Why?" I asked. She said it was a bad sign for an emperor to have a "damaged" offspring. She became a shame to the family. I could feel tears welling up in my eyes. "Why is she in south Dhaka?" Eanna answered with an embarrassed tone, "It was not supposed to go that way, but it is done."

"Let me be straight with you," I said. "I want to save this girl and give her a real home." Eanna looked at me and said, "If you take Bashiri, it will cause a problem, right now she is invisible, can't you save another child? I could see Eanna was upset too.

I looked down into my Merlot and said, "I thought we were going to be roommates."

It was at that point everything changed. Eanna said, "If you want to do this we have to do it right." I can't remember when a smile took my face so quickly.

I knew on the spot we were sisters. A roommate is a lesser thing. I told her about Venki's idea to go to Russia en route to America. Her head bounced back and forth. She said, "There is some merit there. But there could also be trouble." "Really!" I said, "Stealing a child and taking her behind the iron curtain could be trouble?" I said with great doubt and sarcasm in my voice. Eanna looked at me and said in a Walter Cronkite voice, "There is no more iron curtain." I thought she is right; people fly to Moscow the same way they fly to Paris these days.

"What do we do?" I said. She said, "First you have to learn the language." I stood up and said, "Let me take you to your new apartment." We paid the bill and left.

All Eanna had was one suitcase. "I travel light" was her smiling answer. She unpacked and I made some spaghetti. As the night rolled on she began teaching me the basic structure of the language. It was difficult; Bangla is more like an Indian language than a romantic one, like French or Spanish. Still, over the next few weeks, we worked hard, I mean hard. After week two we did not speak a word of English unless absolutely necessary. We were really growing closer. I began to see a beautiful character in Eanna. She is the type of friend you would love to have forever. After the last lesson, on day 18, I said in Bangla, "I want to go and talk to Bashiri." She nodded in a knightly sort of way and we vowed to make the trip in the morning.

Chapter 27
WE HAVE TO GET OUT OF HERE.

As we pulled up on my scooter, I felt like the queen of England. The fact that Eanna was holding on with white knuckles counting her rosary was not evident to me. I got off the scooter and ran to the door. As usual, smoke was coming from within. I knocked and nobody was home. I thought to myself, if this were a movie, I would have to delete this scene, how anti-climatic. I was just thinking how I was so self-proud when I heard a sound. It was barely audible, just a whimper. It was from within. It was then I realized the smoke coming from within was not the smoke of a stove or barrel, this smelled like a real fire.

I went through that door with such speed, as I have never known. The woman I thought I was from a life before was gone forever and I was here flying into a burning house. There was smoke everywhere. But where was Bashiri? I looked and looked until I was coughing so much I had to go outside.

I told Eanna what was going on and she ran into the burning house as if her own child was inside. Eanna covered her face with a fleece to protect her from the flames and smoke and went from room to room. She found her, in a room almost engulfed in flames. She was in a chair with her arms taped behind her, and ironically had tape across her eyes. Eanna went to Bashiri but was soon was succumbed by the smoke. She wrapped the fleece around Bashiri's head and ran out. She collapsed at my feet. In a broken voice she said, "She's in the back room." I don't think I really heard the last word; I was already running back into the house. When I found Bashiri, her hair was on fire and she was screaming. I grabbed her and with every ounce of my strength, I carried her out of that house. In seconds the house collapsed into a massive inferno. Eanna looked at me and said, "We have to get out of here. This was meant to be a murder."

Now there were three people on my scooter. Except for the seriousness of this event, I bet this would have looked a bit comical. We cruised toward downtown. I pulled in front of my apartment.

Bashiri was sobbing. As we entered my apartment I tried to console her. Thankfully Eanna spoke fluent Bangla. I could hear the love in her voice. I think now, as I remember back, that was one of the most amazing moments of this adventure. The fact that this woman could come into my life in one day and great things like this were happening.

Chapter 28
WE ARE WILLING TO RISK OUR LIVES.

I made some beans and rice and we ate. Eanna told me that Bashiri had said that she always had known that the woman who lived there "as" her mother and the boy who was her brother were not her real family. But she added that she also knew that it was common here to live with another family as your own.

Eanna cut Bashiri's hair in a way to get rid of the burnt part, but still looked pretty. I told her so in English and I knew she understood, then I told her in Bangla and the expression was the same. This is proof that people understand tone as much as they understand content.

I asked Eanna to ask Bashiri if she knew she was the Prime Minister's daughter. A puzzled look came over Bashiri's face and the answer was clear. As the night went on I learned that she was taken from the high-level family shortly after birth. So the disgrace of a damaged child would not tarnish the family name. "How horrible," slipped from my lips.

Over the next few days, there was great fun. We ate constantly and played games. And most importantly, Bashiri was very present and helpful in my learning of Bangla. Sometimes when I was practicing certain conjugations and messing up word groups, Bashiri would say, "no."

You see, she was learning little bits of English at the same time. On day three after we put Bashiri to bed, I cornered Eanna and asked what the relationship was with all these things going on. She nodded as if she needed a confession.

She said, "It all started by you asking the cab driver from the airport where you should stay. That hotel, well it is a mob hotel; that is why it is so nice. When the front desk lady led you to Venki, it was all part of a plan. You should know that Venki is not a bad man, but he is part of the mob." Then she smiled and said, "Do you really think he drives the school bus?"

"But," I said in a halted and fearful voice, "Venki recommended you, so where are you in this web?" She smiled sweetly, then pulled out a large caliber pistol and began polishing it with her blouse. Smiling she said, "Well, I'm not a school teacher." Then she stopped moving, her face slowly rising to meet my eyes. I could see tears in her eyes. She said, "I believe you are doing the right thing, so does Venki. And we are willing to risk everything, maybe even our lives, to help you."

I tried to form a word for what seemed like minutes. I could feel my mouth moving to form the word, but I was trembling and had no breath. Finally, it came forth in a whisper. "Why?"

Eanna started talking about her family and what really mattered in the world and then just went quiet for a moment. Then she said, "There are just not many people like you in this world anymore. And when you came along, it made us all rethink our lives." She looked at me and said something that I believe to this day. She simply said, "I am on your side."

I held her for what seemed like forever. We laughed and cried in each other's arms. Afterward, we agreed to make a real plan the next day and went to bed.

Chapter 29
SHE HELD ON FOR DEAR LIFE.

I woke at the crack of dawn and went into the kitchen to prepare a meal for my new family. I was happily makin' bacon and fryin' eggs when Bashiri walked in. It is amazing to me when I witness a person who is blind — that they are not absent in that competency, they simply overcome it with another. She was saying my name over and over, and using the echo time to find obstacles. I ran over and hugged her. Her arms flew around me with an intensity I did not expect. She held on for dear life. It occurred to me that maybe she didn't get hugged very often.

As I was dropping bread into the toaster, Eanna came in wearing the same clothes as the night before. Well of course, I thought, what else was she supposed to wear? I realized at that moment that we were about the same size and said to her, "After breakfast, I will get you into some clean clothes.

We ate in silence, as we all were quite hungry. It was amazing to me that Bashiri would softly hum as she ate as if it made her so happy she might somehow sing along with the meal.

I took Eanna back to my bathroom where she got a shower and fresh clothes. I think she looked better in them than me. I could see the authentic spark of gratitude in her eyes.

She said, "I have a plan." We all sat down at the table and I said, "Is this something Bashiri should hear?" Eanna just shook her head and said, "It's her life, what do you think?" I just nodded; I knew I was in with the right crew.

As the next few hours went by we discussed logistics and money and timing. In the end she convinced me it was best to go to the Soviet Union, or Russia, I guess, for the next phase.

We called Venki but got his phone mail. Eanna just said that that was normal. I just rolled my eyes. I knew Venki too; at least I thought I did. We got a call back around 11:00 a.m. He said he was through with the school bus route. I said, "I thought you said, he didn't drive the bus?" She said, "I said he was in the mob, of course he does something." I had to laugh. We agreed to meet at a restaurant north of the city square. I was a beautiful day and we ate outside. As usual, Venki was late. We decide to go ahead and order. It was a Greek restaurant and I wasn't really sure what to order, especially here. Eanna told me to get moussaka. I was quite pleased. We all got the same thing but who cares, especially Bashiri who was humming with delight. As Venki walked in, Eanna got up out of respect as if he were her superior. He motioned her to be seated and sat down smiling.

After we finished eating we started the plan. I started with a lot of questions, like how did Venki know the Prime Minister so well? And how could he have not known of the murder attempt? He was quiet but not nervous. He looked up and said, "Why do you think I put you in touch with Eanna." In that moment it became clear to me. Venki knew everything; he could just move the pieces around a little if he wanted to. He knew Eanna was strong and capable.

"Okay, I get all that, but..." I stumbled and looked inward. You know that feeling when you start a powerful sentence or idea and then at the critical moment you can't finish it? Well there I was. I was sitting there with my mouth open but nothing was coming out of it. Then Venki said, "It is not just you." He put his head into his hands and attempted to hold back emotion. He looked up holding himself together and said, "Bashiri does not deserve this." And looked at Eanna and said, "and we are tired." Eanna chimed in and said, "We have been waiting for someone like you; at least I have. Someone who could give us moral conscience to get the hell out." I sat back stunned. "What do you mean."? Venki leaned in and said quietly, "What we mean is if we get caught we will all be killed."

Chapter 30
WE MUST GO TO ESTONIA.

Well that called for a long breath and slow release. They were both looking at me. "Okay, what is the plan?" Both of them lit up, especially Venki. I could see his eyes dashing from side to side. He was biting his lip from anticipation. From nowhere I yelled, "What is it?"

He smiled quietly and leaned back in his chair as if he enjoyed the moment when he knew and we didn't.

"We need some wine," he announced in that kingly Russian accent. In an instant, the waiter was there with his favorite wine. I was beginning to see the rest of the puzzle. It also occurred to me that they were the Bourgeoisie here, so to speak, and they were risking their lives and leaving that behind to help a little blind girl. I felt gratitude on a scale that I had never felt before.

Venki cleared his voice. There was no doubt he was in charge here. He leaned in like a spy movie and said, "I have tickets for all of us to Tallinn. We must go to Estonia first to avoid detection." Brilliant I thought. Then with the same brain I said, "Where's Estonia." Everybody laughed as if I was kidding and I did not feel like giving my western idiotship away.

Then he dropped the bomb. "We leave tonight."

I thought to myself, "Man, I was just starting to like my apartment." Then my internal monologue kicked in and informed me that Venki's brother,

Vanki, probably would not be coming after me for back rent. From nowhere I said with affirmative vigor, "Let's get our shit together."

Which made Bashiri clap and say "shit" loudly. As I smiled, I found myself thinking, "That's my girl." We laughed and swilled our wine and agreed that Venki would pick us up in the cab at 9:30 p.m. The flight was at 11:00.

We had to pack light. Eanna had no choice. I guess Bashiri did not either though I was imagining her in all sorts of outfits that I would buy for her. So basically, it was my suitcase.

We all showered and ate, and began the wait for Venki. You'll never guess what, he was late. But after some time went by we started to get really scared. Just at the moment we decided to go back inside there was a screech of tires and a cab rolled to a halt. "Get in," Venki said with a roar, he was covered in sweat. As we got in I said, "What is it?" Venki hit the gas and said, "They know Bashiri did not die in the fire. The provincial family is afraid the media will find this and exploit it."

We all sat silently in the cab as we drove to the airport. As we entered the facility Venki passed back three envelopes. In each were our fake papers. Everything…Passports, Visa documents, all with fingerprints and photos. My mouth opened to ask the question how, but I never did. I also realized, Venki had not asked me for any real money yet. We parked in a remote lot and Venki started in with what would be our story. He handed me a wedding band and said in a thick Russian accent, "I wish this could be more romantic, but you are now my wife." He looked to the back seat; you are both our daughters, Eanna you are adopted. Thankfully we needed a little laughter. I'm not sure Venki thought it was funny that he had to inform us that a black woman could not be our child yet he laughed just the same. As I surveyed the papers I thought they looked extremely professional. I thought to myself, "I guess we'll see."

As we exited the cab I said to Venki, "Don't you need to register your car?" He looked at me as we walked. Eventually, a large smile came across his face. He said, "You don't get it, we are not coming back." And he laughed out loud.

As we entered the terminal main mezzanine, there seemed to be a disproportionate amount of security. Remember, this is a small airport. One uniformed man walked up to Venki. They shook hands and Venki gave him an envelope, I am sure it was money. He smiled and went on his way.

We were all at the gate. I was beginning to feel like we were going to get out of here okay.

We were to begin boarding in about fifteen minutes. Then I heard something. It was a police radio and it was getting closer. I could see the panic in Venki's eyes. He tried to gather us up but just at that moment, we were surrounded by armed security. They had their guns drawn and pointed right at us. Bashiri clung to me; I knew she knew what was going on. There was an exchange of loud accusations in mostly Bangla, and then the cuffs went on.

Eanna, Bashiri and I were taken to another room. Eanna pleaded with the security woman to examine our documents. But she just said, "You are going to jail." There was some questioning but we all held to our story of going home to Estonia.

Chapter 31

INTERROGATION.

We were separated. I told the attendant that Bashiri was blind and the woman looked at me with a look I will never forget. It simply said that she knew who Bashiri was. I think this frightened me more. I was interrogated. Not like on TV, it was formal and gentle. Then I was taken to a cell. There I remained for several days. I thought it wise to say nothing until the normal processes had taken place. I think it was day five. I finally asked the female guard what was going to happen. She looked at me with a vacant expression and said, "You are going to rot." My eyes flew open and I told her I was an American citizen and I just came here to visit a sponsored child. She walked away laughing. I guess she had heard that one before. I think it was day eleven. I tried to start a conversation with the guard. Remember she spoke only Bangla, and I had a 3rd-grade education at best, maybe a vocabulary of 100 words, yet we talked. Women in this country are treated differently than in the western world, so it was not hard for me to make a connection. I asked her about her home life, her children, if she believed in God. Within minutes she was leaning into the bars telling me of her son that was killed in an accidental drowning, we held hands and cried together. From that day forward I had special treatment. I was able to spend much more time outdoors reading, and I got better meals. I think this went on for about three months. I had sent a letter to the American consulate, but I did not know if it was ever really sent. The letter explained my situation and how the predicament that I have found myself in has landed me in prison. Well, I guess the letter was actually sent because I got a visit from the consulate himself. I told my story and we talked at length about the possible solutions. He promised he would be back and left to talk to the warden. When he returned he said, "You have a hearing tomorrow. I will be there. I have arranged all the information and I think everything is going to be okay."

Chapter 32

NINTIA.

Well, tomorrow came but no consulate, then the next day and the next. I had been talking to the female guard I had befriended, her name is Nintia, pronounced Neen-cee-a. She said that the consulate had been arrested. "Oh God," I cried, he was my only hope. Nintia said she thought there was another way. We made eye contact the way only women can do. It was to the bone. She also said there was a young blind Bangladesh girl who wanted to see me. Tears filled my eyes as I was reintroduced to hope. "When," I yelled unabashedly. "How about now?" Nintia said with tears in her eyes too. I found my head uncontrollably nodding with an enormous grin on my face. I was placed in handcuffs as is standard and led outside to another building. The sun felt great on my face. I thought for the first time that maybe there was a happy ending to this part of the journey. This building was very different than the place where I was held. Nintia took off my handcuffs and said, "Stay very close." There were children here. I started getting shaky at the idea of a regime that would imprison children. Nintia told me that this was not prison but a holding place for them. My shoulders fell a bit. We walked down the corridor and I saw the broken part of humanity in little pieces every few feet. Finally, I let out a yell, "Bashiri!"

It took about one second for the call to return, "Julia!" If I have ever felt my heart, it was at that moment. I will never forget that moment. I started running, this is not something you do in a detainment center. I heard a shout from Nintia, and then a shot rang out. That is all remember.

Chapter 33
I THINK I'VE BEEN SHOT.

I woke up in the infirmary. If you can call it that. It stank and there were flies everywhere. And there were cots scattered about — maybe fifteen women in here. There was a searing pain in my right shoulder. As I came to, I could see it was covered with gauze. I tried to let out a yell, but all that came forward was a whisper. I tried to move and then my yell finally came, as a pain as I have never felt before. Slowly a large woman approached me dressed as a nurse. There was comedy here; the nurses' outfit was several sizes too small for her. Sadly, I could not summon a smile. She said something in Russian. "English?" I said hopefully. "What is the matter," she said with a thick accent. I looked up with a straight face and said, "I think I've been shot." The woman exploded into uncontrollable laughter. I guess I kind of get it now. She bent over and in a kind voice said, "You ran from the guards, don't do that." I nodded like a moron.

The days went by like weeks. Imagine lying in a stinky bed surrounded by moaning bodies with nothing to read, no one to talk to, and pain that tests your will to survive. After a week I moved into a room with a radio. This was wonderful. There were only four other women in the room and one spoke English. Plus the radio was helping me with my Bangla and although the music was not of my choosing, sometimes any music is better than no music.

My arm still hurt like hell. On day three a doctor came in. This is the first time I had seen one here. He spoke to the nurse. This nurse was a kind lady and although she spoke very poor English we had created a friendship. She came over to me with a smile. She leaned in and with a sweet tone said, "Doctor must cut off arm." She kept talking but I went into a panic. "No," I screamed. "I am an American." The doctor looked up. He walked to the nurse and muttered some instructions; she smiled. Later she approached me with a giant grin on her face. "You are getting antibiotics." She clapped her hands as if this were some kind of proclamation. I looked up kind of dreary and just said "Good."

After a few days, I started to feel better. I was also taken into a private room, which made me nervous. But I must say the food got much better and I was able to sleep at night. On day four in the new room, the doctor came in alone. We sat in silence for what seemed like a century. Finally, he spoke. "I know who you are." I paused as I collected my thoughts and said, "I hope that is not a bad thing." He smiled. I could feel my shoulders fall; I was very scared. He held his finger over his mouth in the universal signal of talk quietly.

In the next few minutes, he told me that Bashiri and Eanna were okay and that Venki had disappeared. "Where is Venki," I said with sudden and uncontrolled emotion. "I don't know said the doctor. He introduced himself as Dr. Ivan with a very Russian sounding last name and sat there in silence as he undid his shirt. My heart fell until I saw what he was doing. He had a tattoo of the Statue of Liberty on his chest. I just nodded and gave my best smile.

He said he knew about the conspiracy to cover up the birth of Bashiri and then bowed his head and said, "and the murder attempt." "What can we do?" I whispered. "I need to get the three of you out of here but now is not the time. You need to get better to travel and I must make a plan." "Finally," I thought, "a man who can take care of me and make the plans." I was instantly asleep and dreamed of Bashiri.

In this dream, we were floating in a cloud. I could see her smiling face and she could see me. She started moving her arms as if to swim through the cloud and passed by me with a grin, we both laughed. But then she was getting farther away, so I called to her but she was already too far away. I tried to use my arms in the cloud in the same way to catch up but it did not work for me. As I lost sight of Bashiri, I could feel myself slipping through the cloud like I was falling, that's when I awoke.

Chapter 34

AM I GOING INSANE?

I believed that Dr. Ivan had moved me to a better part of the hospital. I enjoyed the better food and the company. But Dr. Ivan seemed to vanish. I asked the women in the room if they remembered his visit, they said no. When I asked the nurse, she said that they had no Dr. with Ivan as a first or last name. Dear God, did I imagine this? Am I going insane? It seemed so real. As several days went by, I started to really doubt my sanity. Sometimes I would wake up in the middle of the night panting, covered with sweat and not knowing why.

As the weeks went by I realized I must have imagined Dr. Ivan out of necessity. I was healthy again and I was afraid to rock the boat because I liked the room, the company and the food. Then it occurred to me. Was I being set up? This was not like prison life. This was a rather nice, if sequestered, existence. Then some things started adding up. I had noticed when I woke up in a panic; the other women were not in the room. I had not really thought about it much because this is prison; people get moved around all the time. But in the morning everyone is back for conversation and breakfast.

I questioned my sanity again. Today would be different. When the nurses came in, and let me say, these women were not dressed as guards. They were nurses yet I was completely well. I had a different point of view and I was ready to risk my comfort.

I jumped up. "What the hell is going on here?" they smiled and said that they were there to deliver breakfast. "This is prison for God's sake, why am I getting breakfast in bed?" there was a moment of discontent. They looked at each other for some sort of confirmation. Then they walked out without a word, sadly with the breakfast.

To my amazement, the other ladies got up and walked out too. I realized now that this had been a strategy to hold me quietly. I started believing in my sanity again and I started believing in Dr. Ivan. Well, nothing happened for several hours, I was getting really hungry and yelled for the nurses, no one came.

I started thinking about a plan for escape. I knew I may have never actually seen Bashiri here, but I heard her voice. I knew it was her, she sounded strong and okay. Now escaping from behind a locked door is a complicated process, and frankly may seem a little futile, but I had all the time in the world.

Here were the facts as I could see. I was being deceived. I did not know why, but I could not trust anybody except maybe Dr. Ivan if he were to reappear somehow. Next, I cannot attack anyone or I will be shot. I can't run or scream for help. So what is left?

A wry smile came across my face. I knew I had to be smart here. How would this go if I decided to work with them? My decision was to stay quiet until I was in the audience of someone that would listen to my plan. Two days went by with no food. I could get water from the sink, but I was getting weak very fast. As I came to consciousness on the third day I went to the door and found a small box. Inside there was the ring I had seen on Dr. Ivan's hand. I began to weep as I began to believe that this meant he was dead. As my trembling hands examined the box, I discovered there was a removable underside. It's not something you would notice without a deliberate search, it kind of slid to the side but you would have to experiment to discover this. Inside there was a small piece of paper folded many, many times. My heart was racing as I unfolded it. Dear God, it was Dr. Ivan. He had bribed a nurse to deliver it to me as a burial present.

The note was cryptic, so as if to be found by another individual it would not make sense. It was a blending of English slang, Bangla, and Russian profanity separated by lots of useless punctuation. I created a deciphering method and found this: June 17.

What did that mean? Was Dr. Ivan going to break us out on that date? Was I going to be executed on that date? Well, I chose the former to believe in and to anticipate.

Chapter 35
THE ESCAPE.

Days past. It was hard to keep a calendar, but the nurses had returned and food was presented to me daily. Unfortunately, the other women were gone. So I was alone all day, every day.

I made little marks on the wall to show the days. The 17th was tomorrow.

An alarm sounded. This had become my life. Alarms were like someone honking their horn in the real world, mostly invisible to me now, but not this one.

Dr. Ivan appeared at my door in civilian clothes. He had a key and opened the door and said, "Let's go now."

He had brought clothes for me. He shouted again, …"now!"

I am not a proud woman and I did not give a damn who was looking as I changed into what felt like …well it's not cotton …it might be someone's imagining of what western clothes might feel like. They felt like plastic. Again, I did not care.

Before I knew what was happening we were moving quickly down poorly illuminated halls. He whispered, "Don't say anything, and pretend you are so sick you can't speak."

Well, the truth was I wasn't too far from that so I nodded to comply.

I softly whispered to him, "Why are you doing this?"

His response will stay with me forever. He said, "If my life can finally stand for something good, I am willing to do whatever it takes."

I knew I could trust this man. As I started to ask him how this was all going to work, he said, "shut up and just go."

Sometimes when your inner monologue tells you — what you have just heard — is what you must do, it comes to you in a very vivid way.

Then there was an explosion. Very loud, the kind you feel to the bone. I dove to the ground. My ears were ringing; I couldn't hear what Dr. Ivan was saying. But his gestures said get up we're going.

As we ran at the end of the hall, I saw hope.

In was Venki. Tears were streaming down my eyes as I ran.

The door had been blown open.

Now, there are things that we can believe in this world. And I guess there are things that we can't. But there it was …a freakin' school bus to help us escape out of prison. And a smiling Russian to drive.

But there was a big problem. We didn't have Bashiri.

As the alarms raged on, I could see people mobilizing. We were not just going to drive out of here. I screamed, "Where is Bashiri?"

As Venki's enormous eyebrows furrowed he said, "She is on the bus."

I looked and she was waving to me as if she saw me clear as day.

I could hear Dr. Ivan shouting, "Let's go" when a shot ran out behind.

Dr. Ivan fell. He was holding my ankle. I bent over to lift him and he said, "Go now." I looked to Venki and he nodded.

I cried and shouted to Venki. Then in a moment all my own, I knew I could not save everyone. I got on the bus.

Chapter 36
THE AIRPORT.

You know what? You just don't see a school bus pulling up to an airport terminal with three people very often. Well, maybe in Bangladesh. Yet no one looked over and it looked like we were going to Estonia. There were sirens in the background, but there were always sirens in the background. Someone I cared for had just been shot. And maybe even killed, and we were just running away. Sometimes you just have to give it up. Really, what else could we have done? I will have a life to think it over.

I walked with my head held high in my new plastic clothes with my beautiful new daughter.

Oh God, did I say that? Hell yes, and I meant it. An enormous smile appeared on my face. I looked down to Bashiri and I swear she smiled back.

Bashiri and I held hands and Venki led the way. Remember this is not an airport like most of us know. It was dirty, people were smoking and the smell of urine was revolting.

Yet I was about as happy as I had been in a long, long, time.

Things went by the numbers and we were actually on a plane on the runway. Well, we were just sitting there and everyone else must have felt as comfortable as you might feel on any flight. Seconds, minutes, and then an announcement "We have a little issue on this flight, just relax and we will fix it."

I looked at Venki in terror; he was drinking vodka and reading a magazine. What is it with us Americans, why are we so uptight? I started to laugh which made Bashiri laugh.

Finally, we were in the air. It is about a seven hour flight to Tallinn, the capital of Estonia.

As we departed everything seemed wonderful. The people were so friendly and caring. As we approached the terminal, Venki said, "Wait here."

Well, that's when the wonderful ended. As Venki was talking to an airport man a shot rang out. We all ran. Venki seemed okay but he wasn't.

We slipped into a cab and Venki said in Estonian "hospital." It sounded like "Haigla."

I could see now that Venki was bleeding badly. I screamed, "hurry" though I knew the driver probably did not understand me. Finally, we made it, Venki was checked in with the help of some American currency and Bashiri and I just prayed.

Hours went by. Finally, a doctor emerged and said that Venki had taken a bullet in his liver. This was not good and he could not travel. After we asked all our questions we felt that Venki would be okay with time.

Hey, he had waited for us. We decided we would wait for him. We slapped our hands in agreement. She cried and I did too.

I only had about four hundred dollars left so I decided to try to see if Brian could send me some funds. As we spoke he said: "whatever you need." I heard this through silent tears. I wish everyone could have a brother like that. Soon we were in a decent hotel and we could visit Venki daily. He looked okay. I guess the liver is not the best way to take a bullet. But he was jovial.

Besides Venki, I have never known anyone whose definitive characteristic was jovial. That counts for something in my book. We had the tickets to America, but we were waiting.

Two weeks passed. Estonian food is remarkably unremarkable. Don't get me wrong it is good food, just bland. I shouldn't say bland, how about mild.

At last Venki was released from the hospital. He looked good and sounded good.

Chapter 37
THE LAST FLIGHT.

As I spoke with Venki about our flight to America, he was listless. He wanted to stay in Estonia. I raised my hand to slap him but good sense intervened. He raised his tired eyes to me and said, "We will need four thousand dollars U.S. to get to America."

I smiled and said "Okay." As if I held the key to the universe.

Then Venki leaned to me and in a pained voice said, "There is something you should know."

Somehow I knew this was going to be the deal breaker. I shook my head and said "no."

Venki was weeping; he said he loved Bashiri and me.

There was a long silence. Then…

With a long painful breath he said, "I am wanted by the KGB. If I go with you they will follow. You will never be safe."

I exploded into tears. "No, you are coming with us!" I cried.

"Do you have the ring?" Venki said calmly.

He stopped and put his hand on my shoulder. There was a long silence — then he began to speak.

"The ring is a long-lost possession of the Russian elite. Dr. Ivan used it to bribe the guards. Yet we were charged with returning it to Russia before we leave."

He never said another word he just smiled. I tried to ask about the ring but Venki just placed his hand over my mouth. We were not leaving tonight.

Venki was getting better and stronger. The Estonian food must have been a real blessing after I called it bland.

Days went by when we did not talk of the situation. We walked and Bashiri always seemed to love Venki, she loved everyone but especially him. You almost couldn't not love him.

But eventually, I cornered him. "When are we getting out of here?" He looked at me as if I were asking about the weather. "When do you want to leave?" he said.

"Now, damn it." I said as I covered my mouth. A slow wry grin formed on Venki's face.

"Where is the ring?" he asked. "I have it," I whispered as if we were secret agents.

"There is something you should know about the ring." Venki said casually.

"Okay, what?" I think a minute passed. What is it with Europeans that they can just be quiet in a conversation? Americans are always full throttle on hearing their voice and point of view. Despite my inner monologue, more time passed.

Then, "It is a code." Venki said. "What kind of code?" I asked.

"A secret one,'" Venki said. "What is the point of a code if it is not secret?" I yelled.

Venki looked around again as if we were secret agents. He said, "I get it, that's funny."

"I'm not trying to be funny, I am trying to get this girl and you back to the United States."

I was all out of breath and I could feel my pulse rising. "So what should we do now?" I said with all the seriousness I could summon.

Venki took that long breath that meant something bad was about to follow. "You and Bashiri must leave without me. I will follow."

"Why?" I said as tears were beginning to well up in my eyes. He said, "I must deliver the ring myself, don't worry everything will be okay."

The flight to America, which we all had tickets for, was leaving at 1:22 a.m. Somehow it infuriated me that we all had tickets but we were not going together. Bashiri seemed to understand. My life did not give me the emotional tools to survive the way these two took each day, one at a time. I loved them both. And I told Venki that we would do whatever he told us to.

He kissed me on the cheek and he kissed Bashiri too. We both giggled, as we have not been kissed in a while. And that was it. He turned and walked away and we proceeded to the gate.

Chapter 38

I DON'T KNOW HOW LONG I CAN GO ON LIKE THIS.

Once again there was an alarm sounding. People in the U.S. wouldn't get this alarm thing that seems to be omnipresent in Eastern Europe and South Asia. It is really unnerving. Anyway, we walked on. Then, of course, there was another explosion. We hit the ground and I just started crying. Bashiri took my head in her arms and kissed me. "We are going to be alright," she said in terrible English.

I remember thinking "I don't know how long I can go on like this." In the last 24 hours, I can count the horrors most people will not have to face in a lifetime. The good news is, it is thoughts like these that get me back on track again. I cannot give up. There is someone at stake here besides me. And I love her. Oh, and there's Venki too.

As the commotion subsided there was a scary silence. Imagine almost pure silence in an airport and you will get what I mean. Something isn't right.

Then she said it. I was thinking it but I did not want to say it. Bashiri whispered, "We can't leave Venki."

Okay, here comes a life realization again. How can this girl who is hunted, who is blind, be prepared to sacrifice an escape because she loves another person. If I can only learn that lesson, I thought, this will all be worth it.

We collected ourselves off the floor and looked into the unlit hall. "This way," Bashiri said as if she could see the universe. We walked down that dark hall hand in hand and I was not afraid — maybe for the first time in my life. Okay, maybe for just today, but that was good enough for me.

That's how you learn courage, I believe now, by observing it. Especially when it is demonstrated by a six-year-old blind girl.

Okay, maybe she is seven now.

I asked Bashiri when her birthday was and she was silent. I decided not to push it. After about a minute she said, "I don't know."

Look, I am not a weepy person but I just let go.

I said, "Today is your birthday, forever!" In a voice so loud it would surely give us away if we were hiding. But we were not hiding we were walking into whatever destiny held for us, because we were going to find Venki.

Finally, the corridor led to a lit area and there were people and movement. I asked an Estonian official about Venki, he knew nothing.

I swear we searched that entire airport twice and he was gone. We were both really tired. We went back to the hotel. No Venki. We checked in and went to bed. The next day was beautiful; it really is a beautiful country, Estonia, especially in spring.

As the meaninglessness of this set in, I started to panic. Then, astonishingly, there was a knock on the door. My eyes flew open with fear. Bashiri smiled and said. "I wonder who it is?" I guess when you have been in a burning house with tape across your mouth a knock on the door must seem pretty inoffensive.

I took a deep breath and asked whom it was. "Room service," was the answer. We had not ordered any room service. It was Venki, all dressed up as a waiter. "Are you kidding me," I sputtered. He walked in pushing his large cart.

Chapter 39
THE RING.

He was exhausted and looked terrible. But he did bring food! We jumped on it like wild animals. Well, mostly me. Bashiri just smiled and ate slowly.

As we started to get our wits back, I said with no particular expression, "Where have you been?" Venki wiped his brow with the tablecloth. "It has not been easy."

Minutes passed before he spoke again. "I knew they needed the ring, but they wanted to interrogate me."

"What exactly is that ring for?" I asked naively. "Don't ask," was the only reply and I am sure the best one. Venki finally ate and we all slept.

The next morning we showered and prepared to go back to the airport. "It will not be like yesterday," Venki said. "They are looking for Bashiri."

"Who is looking for Bashiri, we are in Estonia," I said. Venki paused and said "KGB."

Fear covered me like a blanket. Bashiri put her arms around me. I started to silently sob. I could not understand why the KGB would be involved in an insane murder attempt in Bangladesh. But maybe it did make sense in an insane world. One that we were trying to escape from.

Venki said, "Don't worry, I have a plan."

There is nothing sexier than a Russian man when he is going to save you and your daughter. All right I said it, she is my daughter and I am going to make it happen even if it kills me, and right now it seems like it just might.

'What's the plan?' I said in a hopeful voice.

He said, "We are going to cut Bashiri's hair to make her look like baby."

I smiled and laughed. "Venki, she is like 70 pounds!"

Venki looked on in that way that made me believe we could do this. He said with some pride, "In Russia, we have some pretty big babies."

He said," They will be looking only for a young blind child, not us."

He started unloading the stuff he had on the waiter cart from the night before. There was a large child carrier unit; I'd guess I'd call it, and large baby clothes. I think Bashiri was excited about how ridiculous this all was and the fact that we might get away with it.

Her hair was beautiful. I hated to cut it, but it was kind of fun, like I was taking care of her. The best part was the 'binky' …at least that's what I call it. Bashiri loved it and squealed with delight. We all laughed out loud for a long time. This was a real gift for us all because we had not had a release like this in a long time.

Seriously, could there be comedy in all of this? When Bashiri was in the large baby clothes I was astonished. Without a close inspection, she looked like a baby, I guess a large one, but still if I could believe it maybe everyone would.

Chapter 40
THE ESCAPE.

Bashiri was strapped to my back like a backpack, her legs tucked up in the clothes to appear small. As we walked out of the hotel, no one even looked. I started to gain confidence. We hopped in a cab and were off to the airport equipped with Estonian currency, and as a bonus, a non-crying baby.

We paid the driver and entered the airport. Everything seemed okay for a while. Then just before we entered security, we saw them. Russian soldiers and they were armed.

Venki said softly, "Just look straight ahead and keep on walking." The soldiers did not notice my heart was about to just beat out of my chest, but amazingly they passed on by. After all, they were looking for a little girl, not a baby.

We turned the corner and we were stopped. These were plain-clothes men. Venki spoke to them in Russian. I began to tremble but knew I had to keep it all together.

One of the Russian men pulled back the hood off Bashiri's head. We had told her to fake slumber the whole time. The Russian said something and he and Venki both laughed. We walked on.

I asked Venki what the Russian said that seemed so scary to me and he responded "big baby." The real beauty about Venki's plan was that they were not only searching for an older girl, they were searching for a blind girl. And everyone appreciates a sleeping baby. Her eyes closed and a secret smile on her face. I loved it.

We boarded the plane without a hitch. When I heard the door hatch close it occurred to me that maybe we were going to make it. Seconds seemed like minutes, but after a while, we were in the air. We were heading for America.

Chapter 41
JFK NEVER LOOKED SO GOOD.

As we descended we talked about next steps. I did not have an apartment anymore, but I did have Brian. As we taxied on the runway I called him. He was totally surprised and dropped a dish; I guess he was cooking something. He said breathlessly "Where are you." Without a thought I replied, "We are right where we need you." I laughed… he did not. "We are in New York." There was a long silence. I finally cut in, "Don't worry, we are alright. I am here with Venki and Bashiri." Silence again. Then, "How can I help?" That was the brother that I remember. "We have money but nowhere to go," I said. Brian paused and said, "Come to number 58 at 72nd and 9th."

We were on our way. We jumped into a cab; the driver was Russian. Can you believe? I smiled with one of those ridiculous smiles and we were rolling.

We were welcomed into Brian's flat. It was small and plain, but it was a welcome site. We knew it was safe and that meant a lot right now. It took Brian about a second to fall in love with Bashiri. They both wept instantly. Venki and I did too. It was about time for a good cry.

Chapter 42
MY BEAUTIFUL BROTHER BRIAN.

We ordered some Chinese takeout. It was pretty good but I could not stop laughing at how Bashiri cheered it. "Best ever," she said. "This girl is going to be easy to please," I thought with a delightful sense of calm. Brian was quiet, just observing. We told our story, at least a little bit of it, and he just stared. "What is it, I asked? He smiled in his beautiful way and said, "There is something I have been meaning to tell you."

At that moment there was a knock on the door. "Perfect." Brian said. He got up and opened the door. Another young man came in smiled at us and hugged Brian.

Brian turned to us blushed with excitement and said, "This is Brian and we are in love."

I covered my mouth and just looked on. Bashiri ran to Brian's Brian and hugged them both. I realized right then that she was a lens to whatever heaven there may be on earth. She had no judgment only instant love. I also realized then that it was I to be the learning one, not she.

I laughed out loud without meaning to. "So you are in love, Brian, with a man named Brian." They both just looked at me, grinning and nodding. Bashiri exclaimed in very poor English, "perfect!" Vanki started applauding and I just said, "Perfect."

The next few days were full of planning and shopping. It was such a delight just to watch Bashiri touching clothes and seeing her grin. I wonder how that sensory perception could be so pleasing. But I was glad it was. She would choose clothes on feel. And it did not matter what they looked like. This gave me a real charge. She was showing me a world of pure contentment, without all the concerns of …what will everybody think. I began to forget the notion of what people think. I was so in tune with Bashiri that she literally could find me in the stores without calling my name. I can't explain it, but it's true.

We had been living with Brian and Brian for about three weeks when Venki suggested we might be wearing out our welcome. "What are we going to do," I asked. Venki looked at me in his caring way and said, "We will find a way." I realized right then, and this is a secret, that I had fallen for Venki long ago. Any man who was willing to rescue an unknown girl, risking his own life, over and over, is already a very special person. For me, it only takes one more click of kindness to send me over the edge. And I was over.

Over in a good way.

I was really surprised how well I was received back in the advertising world. I actually turned down two jobs as I realized I could be a consultant and make enough money and spend more time with Bashiri. I got a short gig with a local agency, and then scored a long-term gig with one of the major agencies. I'm back.

This allowed me to work from home and get Bashiri enrolled in school. Of course, it was a school for the blind, but Bashiri made friends instantly and never complained. In fact, as I look back, she never ever complained. I wonder what we as a culture can learn from that. Seriously, if anyone had it hard you might think she would be a little bit bitter, but she was sweeter than sunshine. Always. And I will go on the record saying that that is not just a mother's opinion. Everyone loves Bashiri. Not just Venki and me.

Speaking of Venki. I'm sure you've guessed. Yes, I love him and he loves me, and of course Bashiri. But what were we going to do about it? Venki said we should wait and figure something out based on our financial situation. I just threw my arms around his neck and said the words I will remember and cherish for a lifetime. "Marry me you big, fat Russian!"

I could see tears in his eyes. He just said, "Okay."

Chapter 43
THE TIGER.

You know when you are shaking your head 'no' when you are trying to be open-minded about something.

That is what I was doing.

"I don't want this," ….I said to myself as I noticed I was shaking my head no again.

Bashiri wants, more than anything, to go sailing.

At the same time, I knew how afraid of water I was… to the bone. Beyond fear.

I rolled my eyes as I thought…is this some kind of exorcism I must endure to completely join with her? Is this what being a parent means?

Well if that is her deepest wish, who am I to cave-in to my fears. So I booked the cruise.

Well, it's not a cruise just a little boat ride. That's what I keep repeating.

Little…boat….ride.

It's funny how things in the future are not really that scary.

But as they approach they are like a tiger. Each day felt a little different.

They were really all the same, sending Bashiri off to school, and me crafting my consulting business. Yet, …there was the tiger, silently closing.

Then, the boat ride was tomorrow. I remember thinking this tiger metaphor is ridiculous. Yet, I swear I could feel the hot breath on my neck.

As I said the words out loud, I could feel the presence. I made a promise not to project negative energy.

As I made the oath, I was clearly projecting negative energy. I was shaking my head no again.

Zero hour.

It was Tuesday and sunny. Everyone at the pier was smiling.

I was too… but one of those "everyone knows you're not happy" smiles.

Bashiri was already everyone's best friend. I loved her for that. It made me smile.

"This is going to be ok," I started saying over and over in an unconvincing mantra.

Bashiri could feel the stinging mist on her face and squealed, "Permission to come aboard." Her English was excellent.

At last, we were at sea.

Alas, we were at sea. Deep swallow and deep breathing.

The Captain was named Jamel. He had bad breath on a rather global scale and BO that could start a rebellion. Really. As he flashed his brown teeth, I just wondered how this could be a movie somehow.

By the way, Bashiri thought the captain was awesome. I am sure, really sure, that in her mind's eye he was Captain Ahab.

I sat down and started the prayer I use when I am taking off in a plane. It starts off with the Lord's Prayer, and then ends up with please don't let me die now.

As we sailed out of the bay, I knew this was love. I would not do this for anyone else. This was for Bashiri. That thought made me feel safe and whole.

What seemed like hours went by. I asked old Ahab when we were heading back. He looked surprised and said we had not reached open water yet.

Great. Great.

Yup, that is what I said, over and over.

Is it ever cool to throw up?

Now I know the answer.

Luckily, Bashiri was up at the front of the boat with Ahab, and I was free of embarrassment.

No stains, gladly.

Not on my clothes, but on my heart. I felt like I had to abort, to scream for help and end this.

I tucked my hands under my legs and rocked back and forth. I suddenly knew every cell in my body was in total rebellion.

After a time. Let's say it was a few minutes. It may have been seconds.

I felt better. I felt myself nodding 'yes'… It made me smile to myself.

Bashiri was still up front with the captain. We were picking up speed and it seemed strangely exciting. I felt strong again.

So with a grin like I just scored a touchdown, I rose to greet this moment and try to reach for Bashiri's joy in all of this.

Then.

The boat shuddered violently.

My newfound strength instantly evaporated.

As I rushed to Bashiri I was washed with the desire to hold her and tell her how much I loved her.

As I ran, everything suddenly switched to slow motion.

I tried to turn my head, but for some reason, I could not. Voices were around me but I could not hear what they were saying.

Then I knew.

I was in the water.

Somehow, I was hit by the boom and I knew it was over.

I can't swim and I was terrified.

I didn't want to die and…

…now, I guess I was

…going to die.

As I took a mouthful of water I yelled,"Bashiri!"

I don't know what happened next except for what I have been told.

Darkness.

You see; blind people don't dive into the water.

Not for anything.

But.

But, that is what happened that day.

As Jamel, or Ahab, or whatever yelled for her to stop, she dove immediately when she heard me scream.

Blind people can locate sounds with great acuity. Not like us.

I could feel my arms flapping as I started to slip. Like cinder blocks were pulling me down.

I knew I was done, …so with my last breath I softly said….Bashiri. I was smiling.

I went under. Everything went black and cold.

For no reason, I suddenly remembered a hidden memory of my father swinging me as a child. Everything was in black and white.

Then.

Then, I felt a strong presence. I opened my eyes and it was Bashiri.

She had somehow found me and was pulling me up.

As I looked at her I knew she could see me too.

That is the last thing I remember before waking up in the hospital.

As I opened my eyes I saw the saw-tooth grin of Ahab.

But I heard a squeal of joy from beyond. It was Bashiri.

And I could feel Venki holding my hand.

I closed my eyes and knew everything was going to be okay.

The end.

To Bangladesh with Love is a work of fiction.

As a special gift, though I would like to give you two actual letters not penned by me, this is the real thing.

There is another book coming entitled *Bashiri*, where we find out she is not only entitled to political power in Bangladesh, but untold fortunes and much more. Yet as you will see it is precisely her disfigurement — and the sheer desire from others to destroy her out of embarrassment, that reveals her to be the person that possibly can save us all.

Here are the two letters as they were originally written later in life:

From Julia to Bashiri

Bashiri,

You are such an amazing child.

You saved my life. I was looking for something I couldn't see - some purpose beyond what I was doing in my life. I have no doubt my heart led me to you.

You are filled with bravery and courage. So much that it makes other people like me strive to be the same. You are a light in this world. I want you to never feel afraid; but if you do, believe in yourself and know that you will be okay. Do not run from fear. You are a gift of life and it will carry you through anything both good and bad.

You have changed everything for me and I am forever grateful to you.

You may have blindness of your eyes but not your heart. For you can see so much more than anyone because you see through your heart.

That is your gift Bashiri.

The gift you bring to the world.

Love,

Julia

From Bashiri to Julia:

Julia,

You are the person who saved my life.

I have no doubt.

In a place where I find I can't find anything to say, here are 3 things I know for sure:

1. FAITH

Faith is when you really trust something you cannot see. This is something I read a long time ago that I believe, "It is when you trust, absent of knowledge, that you just know something and you blindly follow or go in that direction. It's a place you can feel but yet cannot see."

I believe you can sometimes see what others may not or cannot see because their minds will not let them.

Let them see kindness and grace through a source of inner strength to help them believe in themselves and believe they can get there. Wherever "there" is for them.

You can help them find what I call their "North Star"...their special place in the universe.

2. FORGIVENESS

Someone once told me to never doubt the power of forgiveness.

That is in forgiveness you have nothing to lose and everything to gain.

That "everything" is your life.

So, forgive. It gives you space to live.

Let go. It gives you even more space to live.

Then discover your life purpose and fill that space with who you are at the very core. And then feed it, nourish it and grow it by sharing it with others who will fill it up over and over.

3. LOVE

Be present.

Be in the moment.

And just love people for who they are. We're all trying to do the same thing…to be the best person possible.

When you meet people for the first time or look at them during really hard times, always remember this.

We are all trying to be the best person we can be at that moment in time.

I love you Julia,

Bashiri

About the Author

Andrew is an award-winning writer and human behaviorist. With a long history in the advertising world, he understands the human condition and has written several papers on human truth.

Andrew and his wife live near Memphis with a yellow lab named Blue.

Andrew is the one on the right.